BEN'S GIFT

Cynthia Barnett

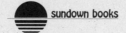

ATTENTION READERS: We would like to hear what you think about our books. Please send your comments or suggestions to:

The Editors
Signal Hill Publications
P.O. Box 131
Syracuse, NY 13210-0131

• • •

This book is fiction. The author invented the names, people, places, and events. If any of them are like real places, events, or people (living or dead), it is by chance.

SIGNAL HILL

© 1990 Signal Hill Publications
A publishing imprint of Laubach Literacy International

10 9 8 7 6 5 4 3 2

ISBN 0-88336-210-4

Illustrations by Christine Bahouth
Cover design by Chris Steenwerth
Cover photo by Dave Revette

Signal Hill is a not-for-profit publisher. The proceeds from the sale of this book support the national and international programs of Laubach Literacy International.

PRINTED WITH
SOY INK™

This book was printed on 100% recycled paper which contains 50% post-consumer waste.

Chapter 1

Ben had just awakened. It was his first morning at the boarding house. At least this was better, he thought. Better than Rest Haven. Nothing could be as bad as that. A nursing home at 37! He'd rather be in a boarding house any day.

Ben was born with cerebral palsy. Part of his brain had been damaged somehow. He was lucky it was not the learning part. But he had problems moving his muscles. He could not walk alone because his legs were too stiff. His arms were better. Still, they often refused to obey his brain.

Around the house, Ben used a walker. It was slow, though. He also had a folding wheelchair. That was mostly for going out. He didn't use it much.

Ben had trouble with his speech. He had to speak slowly. Even so, he was sometimes hard

3

to understand. This was frustrating for him. He liked being with people, and talking to them. But few would take the time and trouble to listen to him.

He lay in bed and looked around. His room was small. Just as well, Ben thought. It was easier to get around.

Getting from the bed to the table was no problem. From table to dresser it was a big stretch. But, once he made it to the dresser, the rest was easy.

Satisfied, Ben relaxed. He could get to the bathroom without help. Getting into the tub, of course, was another matter. Maybe Chuck would help.

Ben tensed at the thought of Chuck. Ben could not forgive his younger brother. Chuck had it all: a wife, two kids, and a job. And Chuck had a house.

But Chuck didn't want Ben. I don't want Chuck's help, anyway, Ben thought bitterly. I won't ask Chuck for anything. I'll learn to get by on my own.

For 37 years, Ben had lived at home. He hadn't been able to go to school. He had learned basic skills from a tutor.

Because of his handicap, Ben needed a lot of help. His mother gave it to him gladly. She also made Chuck do a lot for Ben. She meant well, of course. But she had done too much.

All that had changed now. Ben's mother had died two and a half months ago. Ben stayed in a nursing home until Chuck found a room for him to rent. Yesterday, Chuck had helped him move into the boarding house. And, now, the day had come. Ben was on his own.

Distracted by the sound of a passing plane, Ben looked up. He could see the top of a tree through the window. The leaves were almost all yellow.

Beyond the tree, the sky was blue. September was almost over. The breeze from the window was cool and fresh. It almost seemed to hold a promise. With all his heart, Ben hoped it did.

* * *

It took Ben a long time to get dressed. Then, using his walker, he went into the hall. He crossed the living room carefully. The room was full of furniture. Even worse, the tables were covered with knickknacks. Ben knew how easily he might knock them off.

Ben tried to keep his arms at his sides. Somehow, he did it. Relieved, he entered the dining room. The table was bare.

At home, it had been different. He had slept until he woke up. When he was ready, his mother cooked whatever he wanted. As he stood there, thinking of his mother, Mrs. Brandon came in.

"Well, good morning, Benny," she greeted him loudly. "You're a real sleepyhead this morning. Didn't you hear me say that breakfast was at seven? I'm just finishing up the dishes now. I can't cook three different breakfasts, you know."

"I'm sorry," Ben mumbled. "I'll wait until—"

Mrs. Brandon didn't seem to hear. She went right on talking.

"But come on and sit down, Benny. I'll make you some toast."

"Well, I wouldn't want to—" Ben started.

"Now, don't worry, honey," Mrs. Brandon said. "I'll take good care of you."

Ben sat. He didn't think he had much choice.

Mrs. Brandon brought the toast. Then, she sat down next to him. He wanted to escape, so he tried to hurry. As usual, it didn't work. At times like this, his hands seemed to ignore his brain. Sure enough, the butter he meant for his toast wound up on his shirt.

Clucking with pity, Mrs. Brandon buttered the toast for him. At last, she sensed Ben's embarrassment. She began talking about her husband, who had died five years ago.

After breakfast, Ben went back to his room. Mrs. Brandon is something else! he thought. At least she had rented him a room. Chuck had tried five other places first. No one wanted Ben. One person was too busy. Two other rooms were suddenly filled. But to Ben, the message was the same: You're different. You bother us.

Chapter 2

Ben was not late to lunch. In fact, he was the first one there. He wondered what the other boarders were like. There were two of them, Harold Greer and John Fuller. John worked at the local mill. Harold was "job hunting." Mrs. Brandon had shaken her head when she told Ben this.

As Ben sat down, Mrs. Brandon came in to set the table.

"Well, Benny, you sure took off fast this morning. I was going to ask you to help me fold some laundry. What have you been doing all morning?"

"Reading," Ben answered shortly.

"Reading!" exclaimed Mrs. Brandon. "How wonderful that you can read! Well, that certainly must help to pass the time."

Ben smiled weakly. Same old story, he thought. People were often surprised to find that he could read. In fact, it was his greatest pleasure. In real life, Ben's world was small. With a book, Ben could go anywhere, do anything.

A man came in and sat down across from Ben.

"Benny, this is Harold," Mrs. Brandon said.

"Glad to meet you, old chap," Harold spoke heartily. "Welcome to our humble home. Has the Mother Bee been taking good care of you?"

Confused, Ben looked around.

Mrs. Brandon smiled tightly. "Harold finds that little name quite amusing, though I'm not sure why," she said.

Ben didn't know what to say. "You get it, don't you, Benny?" Harold went on. "Capital *B* for Brandon. Make it *Bee* because she's always busy. And also because she has been known to sting!" He smiled smugly.

"Of all the crazy ideas—" sputtered Mrs. Brandon.

Ignoring her, Harold went on. "The *Mother* part is because of her skills at nagging. But you'll soon find that out for yourself."

Ben didn't know what to say. He was relieved when lunch was served. For a while, the three ate in silence. Then, Mrs. Brandon looked at Harold.

"Did you see last night's paper?" she asked.

"Not yet, Mother," Harold said through his teeth.

"Well, you don't have to get huffy! I just happened to read the want ads. There's a job that I thought might interest you."

"For what?" Harold questioned.

"For a night watchman at the mill. I wrote down the name of the person to call." She pulled a piece of paper from her pocket.

"Why, Mother Bee, I'm surprised at you!" Harold said. "What a day for me to go running off. It's Benny's first day. I thought we'd have a friendly chat. We could sit on the porch. It's such a beautiful day."

Mrs. Brandon looked pained. She set the paper beside Harold's plate.

When they had finished lunch, Harold turned to Ben. "What about it, old man? Care to join me on the porch? That is, unless you've got other plans."

"I'd be glad to," Ben replied. After a pause, he gathered his courage and spoke. "But I'd rather be called Ben, not Benny. If nobody minds. Benny was my childhood nickname. I *never* liked it."

"Fine with me," Harold said easily. Mrs. Brandon made no comment. Ben rose stiffly. Slowly, he followed Harold.

Once on the porch, Harold did most of the talking. Ben spoke only to answer Harold's questions. Ben was nervous, so he was glad to sit and listen.

Harold had lived in four different places. New jobs almost every year. He had even been in jail. That shocked Ben, but Harold laughed about it.

"Just some trouble in a bar in Detroit," he said. "Had a few too many, and I lost my head. You know how it is, Ben."

Ben didn't, but he nodded, anyway. He soon felt more relaxed. Harold was easy to talk to. During a pause, Ben asked Harold about his job hunting.

"Mother Bee strikes again," Harold said. "Actually, I'm not looking all that hard. I'll go back to work when I can find the right job. Meanwhile, Uncle Sam gives me enough to get me by. I'm in no big hurry."

Ben was puzzled. He wondered why Harold got money from the government. He didn't want to ask, though. The most confusing thing was about the job. He couldn't see why Harold didn't want one. If *he* could get a job—but, here, Ben had to stop. Ben had never had a job, not a real one. And he doubted if he ever would.

Ben was disturbed by a jab in the ribs. Startled, he looked up. A man was coming down the sidewalk towards them.

"That's him," Harold whispered. "John Fuller. The guy who lives upstairs."

The two men watched John approach. Silently, he walked around to the back entrance. He passed close by, but no one spoke.

"You'll just have to ignore him, Ben," said Harold. "Pretend he's not here. He thinks he's too good for me, and probably for you, too. He doesn't even like to talk to Mother Bee, if he can help it.

"I don't know what he does in that room of his. But we sure never see him around the house. The only time he comes downstairs is to eat. Always comes and goes by the back door. He's a strange one, no doubt about that.

"I used to wonder what he was thinking. Now, I don't even bother wondering. Every now and then, I'll see him when I'm out somewhere. He never speaks, though. Mrs. Brandon thinks that something terrible happened to him once. I think he was just born nasty."

Despite the sun, Ben shivered. He'd be sure to keep his distance from John! At least Harold seemed nice, he thought. And then, there was "Mother Bee." For all her odd ways, Mrs. Brandon had been kind. Well, two out of three's not bad, thought Ben.

Chapter 3

Dinner was a quiet meal. Ben was tense. Before dinner, Mrs. Brandon had introduced him to John. Ben extended his hand, but John just nodded stiffly. He didn't even look Ben in the eye.

Ben was upset. He knew that people were often put off by his handicap. But John seemed shocked. He remembered what Harold had said about John. Still, he found it hard to relax. He was careful not to say anything. He sat down and ate as neatly as he could.

Ben was still eating when John left.

"You mustn't mind John," said Mrs. Brandon. "That's just his way. He's had a tough life, I guess. We never really know what's happened to make people the way they are. We just have to try to accept them. And do our best to get along."

Ben said nothing. Maybe Mrs. Brandon was right. John sure made it hard, though.

Harold pushed back his chair. "See you folks later. I'm off to a meeting," he said. Mrs. Brandon stared after him. Then, she noticed Ben watching her.

"Sorry, Benny," Mrs. Brandon said. "It's just that I know who he's meeting, and where. But it's none of my business, as Harold always reminds me." She stood up abruptly. "By the way, Benny, will you be wanting to watch TV tonight? I'm having some friends over for cards. We usually use the living room. But if you're using it, we could go upstairs."

"It's all right, Mrs. Brandon," replied Ben. "I won't be in there tonight."

Mrs. Brandon smiled her thanks. Then, she rose and began to clear the table.

Ben reviewed his options. The living room was out. He was sick of his room. He thought of calling Chuck, but quickly dismissed the idea. Chuck should have come over by now, Ben fretted. After all, his house was only three miles away. Shrugging his shoulders, Ben started towards the porch.

* * *

The evening air was still warm. Ben could see a long way up and down the street. Across the street, two dogs were playing. Ben could hear someone laughing. Inside the boarding house, Mrs. Brandon was humming. Soon, her friends arrived. They said hello to Ben as they walked up to the door.

Slowly, Ben reviewed the day's events. Harold was nice. Mrs. Brandon was all right. He wondered why she got so mad about Harold's meetings, though. John was—well, a necessary evil. But, best of all, it looked as if Mrs. Brandon would let him stay. Ben was grateful for that.

What would he do all day? He could read and watch TV for only so long. Maybe he and Harold could do things sometimes.

Ben was deep in thought. He didn't notice the little girl at first. She was standing by the fence, in the yard next door. Shyly, she was watching him. Ben guessed that she was four or five years old.

"Hello," Ben called to her.

Eyes on her shoes, she nodded her head.

"What're you doing?" Ben asked.

The child looked up. "What'd you say?"

Ben repeated the question slowly and carefully.

"Nothin'," said the girl. She began to stare again.

"My name's Ben. What's your name?" Ben persisted. He made an effort to speak clearly.

"Susie," she answered.

"Do you live next door?" Ben questioned gently.

Susie ignored the question. "Mister Ben," she blurted, "how come you talk funny?"

Ben felt as if she'd slapped him. It wasn't her fault, he knew. She didn't know any better. It still hurt, though. Suddenly, he felt very tired.

"I can't help it, Susie," he told the girl. "Good night. I'm going to bed." Sadly, he got up and started towards his room.

Chapter 4

The first week passed slowly for Ben. He thought Mrs. Brandon would take him out sometimes. But she complained that his chair was too heavy for her to lift in and out of the car. Besides, she was always in a hurry. She didn't like waiting for Ben.

Harold didn't have a car. He could push Ben's chair, but there wasn't much within walking distance. Ben wished he could get on a bus. It would have been a big help in getting around. But the first step was just too high.

Ben liked talking with Harold. But he had learned not to count on it. Much of Harold's time was devoted to his "meetings."

Sometimes, Harold didn't stay out late. Then, he often came into Ben's room to talk. At such times, it was clear that he'd been drinking. Ben didn't say anything to Harold about it. He didn't want to upset his new friend.

Mrs. Brandon tried to find things for Ben to do. Good old Mother Bee, Ben thought. She was full of ideas, like folding laundry and polishing silver. None appealed to Ben.

Even worse, she was trying to find him a hobby. Ben had to laugh. Her first idea was birdwatching. But Ben wasn't interested in birds. He liked people better.

Mother Bee didn't give up. One day, she went rummaging in her attic. She returned with her son's old stamp collecting set. She had bought it when he was in the third grade. Half of the stamps were already glued in. Mother Bee thought Ben might like to finish it.

Ben was insulted. After all, he wasn't a child. But he was also touched. Mrs. Brandon's son was killed in the Vietnam war. She treated most of his things like treasures. That was why Ben refused. He knew she'd rather keep her son's stamp set the way it was.

Mrs. Brandon also offered Ben the use of her library. At first, this sounded great. But one look at the books changed Ben's mind:

paperback romances, a dictionary, and a Bible. There wasn't one science fiction story in the bunch. He would even have settled for a good detective story.

That was why he agreed to see Chuck. Chuck had called a few days earlier. But Ben had refused to talk to him. He was still mad that Chuck hadn't called right away.

Ben soon regretted his anger. To his relief, Chuck called again. This time, Ben arranged to have Chuck take him to the library the next night.

Ben could hardly wait to get some books. Besides, he had to admit that he missed Chuck. Chuck, Louisa, Bud, and Chip were all the family he had left. And he guessed they were worth forgiving.

Even when Chuck seemed unfeeling, Ben never doubted Chuck's wife, Louisa. She was a warm person, with a loving manner. Bud and Chip were good kids, too. Ben decided he shouldn't deprive them of their only uncle.

The next night, after dinner, Ben went straight back to his room. Let Chuck come to *me,* he figured. Besides, Mrs. Brandon was on the porch. Ben didn't feel like talking to her.

As he waited, Ben glanced around the room. He tried to see it through Chuck's eyes. Pretty shabby, he guessed.

A car door slammed out front. Soon, there was a knock on Ben's door. Both brothers were awkward in their greeting. Chuck got Ben's wheelchair from the closet and carried it to the car. Then, he came back for Ben.

Ben was annoyed, but resigned. He could have made it himself, with the walker. But Chuck didn't like to wait for him. Chuck always carried Ben to the car.

Once on their way, Chuck began the conversation. "How are things going?" he asked.

"Fine. Just great." Ben spoke firmly.

Chuck looked doubtful. "Mrs. Brandon says you don't seem happy," he said.

"That woman!" Ben fumed. "She knows everyone's affairs better than they do. I'm telling you, things couldn't be better. It's just great being on my own."

"Well," Chuck said, "I'm sure glad you like it, Benny. I wonder what you do all day, though. At least at Rest Haven—"

"Damn it, Chuck!" Ben exploded. "Don't ever mention that place again!"

"OK, OK. Sorry, Benny. Though I could never see why you hated it that much."

"Do you really want to know?" Ben asked.

"Sure, I do," said Chuck.

"Then I'll tell you!" Ben fumed. "It made me feel like I was eighty years old. I don't belong in a place like that. So what if I've got CP? I'm still a person, aren't I? Why shouldn't I live like one?"

After this much, Ben had to stop. He was exhausted from talking so much. He glared at Chuck, defying him to argue.

"So you want to be like everybody else," said Chuck.

Ben nodded fiercely.

"Well, everybody else takes care of themselves. Can you do that? Didn't you need the help Mom and I gave you? Can you make it on your own?"

"I can't do everything, Chuck. You know that. But there's a lot I can do."

"Like what?" Chuck asked bitterly. "You never even try. Sure, there are things you could do. But you don't do them. You'd rather have someone else do them for you. And now, there's just me. I can't be your nursemaid anymore. I've got problems of my own. I've got my own life to live."

Ben looked stricken. He and Chuck had never spoken so frankly before. The two men talked little during the rest of the drive. Once at the library, they busied themselves looking for books.

At least I've got some decent books to read, thought Ben on the way home. But his mind

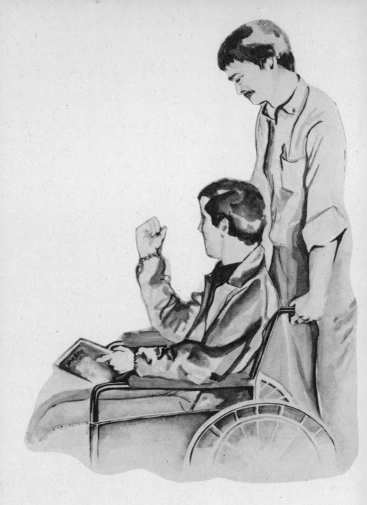

wasn't really on books. He was thinking about his argument with Chuck.

"Louisa and the kids send their love, Benny," Chuck said, at last.

Ben said nothing, but he nodded.

"Louisa wants to know if she can do anything for you."

"Tell her thanks, Chuck," said Ben. "I'm doing all right. How is Louisa?" he asked. He tried to sound casual.

"Busy, as always," Chuck said. "And just as pretty. She never seems to get any older. Oh, I meant to tell you earlier," he added. "Next month is our tenth anniversary. We're going to Hawaii."

"Hawaii!" said Ben, forgetting his anger. "That sounds great! I didn't know when your anniversary was." His mother had always kept track of special days. She bought a present or a card. Then, she would sign Ben's name.

Chuck guessed his brother's thoughts. "We don't want a present, Benny," he said. "We know you're just barely making ends meet."

Ben blushed. Chuck always made him feel stupid. If he wanted to buy a present, nobody could stop him. He'd show Chuck!

After a pause, Ben said, "Maybe what you said earlier was right. Maybe I should try to do more on my own."

Now, it was Chuck's turn to look stricken. "Oh, Benny, I'm sorry! Maybe I was too hard on you. I never meant to say all that."

"It's OK," Ben insisted.

There was an awkward silence.

Chuck pulled up at Mrs. Brandon's and helped Ben to the house. "I'll take you back to the library when you're ready," he said.

Ben thanked him and went into the house.

The idea of a present was still on his mind.

Chapter 5

What could he buy for Chuck and Louisa? The question consumed Ben's thoughts. Chuck had been right about one thing, Ben admitted. He had almost no money to work with. He had two dollars and some change. That was all. There was no hope of any more until the 10th of October. Chuck and Louisa's anniversary was on the 15th. That gave Ben very little time. He'd have to plan ahead. He hoped nothing would go wrong.

After room and board, Ben had about $23 every month. Hardly better than nothing at all, he thought. From it would have to come clothes, toilet articles, and whatever else he needed. Like the daily paper. That would have to go.

After deciding that, Ben returned to the gift. He didn't know where to begin. He'd never been shopping by himself. Ads, he thought. Papers have ads. If I look at the ads, I can decide what to buy. Some stores took phone orders, he knew. Many also made home deliveries. Ben thought it would work.

Then, it hit him. If he cancelled his paper, how could he check the ads? John subscribed,

Ben knew. But that was no help. John was as cold as ever towards him. Harold didn't get the paper.

Mrs. Brandon got the paper. She was his only hope. But Ben didn't want to tell her about the gift. She was such a talker. Ben was sure she'd forget and tell Chuck.

* * *

He waited until dessert. Mrs. Brandon was cutting a cake. Gathering his courage, Ben spoke.

"What do you do with your old papers, Mrs. Brandon?"

"Why, Benny, what a funny question. Why would you want to know?" she said.

Ben squirmed. This was not going to be easy.

"I just wanted to borrow them when you're through," he explained.

"But what about yours?" Harold asked.

Harold, too! I should have told Harold, Ben realized. Now, Ben was embarrassed. He wished he'd waited until John had gone. But it was too late now. Everyone was looking at him.

"I'm going to cancel it. At least for a while. I need to save some money."

Mrs. Brandon looked puzzled. Then, she smiled. "Are you hiding something from us, Benny?"

Ben was startled. How could she know?

Harold spoke up. "Just tuck those feelers right back in, Mother Bee. What if Ben does have a lady friend? It's surely no concern of yours."

Ben choked on his water. So that was what they thought. He could feel his face growing hot. He even saw John holding back a smile. Ben could take no more. He started to get up.

"I'm sorry, Benny," Mrs. Brandon said quickly. "I didn't mean to upset you. You're welcome to my old papers. I'll leave them on the coffee table."

Mumbling his thanks, Ben sat back down. He managed to eat a very large piece of cake.

* * *

Next morning, the paper was on the coffee table. After breakfast, Ben took it to his room. He looked through every page. By the time he finished, he was depressed. Most of the ads were for clothes. Hardly the gift that he wanted. But what did he want?

For almost a week, Ben scoured the papers. He seemed to get nowhere. He began to get edgy. Time was running out! Ben felt disgusted with himself. Couldn't he do even this simple thing?

Ben's depression must have shown. Monday after breakfast, he and Harold were on the porch. Sunday's paper was on Ben's lap. He hadn't had the heart to look at it.

"What's wrong, old man?" asked Harold. "Things can't be that bad."

Ben told Harold the whole story. Harold was eager to help. He even offered to buy the gift for Ben.

"Thanks, Harold," Ben said gratefully. "I've got to do this myself. All my life, people have done things for me. I have to show Chuck I can do this by myself."

Harold understood. He didn't have an idea for a gift, but he did offer to help Ben check the ads. He tried to sound hopeful. Sunday was the best day for ads, he reminded his friend. Ben nodded, but he was not convinced.

Ben flipped slowly through the paper. All the ads looked the same. He still wasn't getting any ideas. Harold whistled as he read. Now and then, he would call out ideas.

"What about a camera, old buddy? Couldn't they use that on their trip?" he questioned.

"I think Chuck has one," Ben said sadly.

"Bet it's not like this," Harold persisted.

"Like what?" Ben asked.

Harold showed him the ad. The camera was tiny. It would fit into a shirt pocket or purse. Ben began to hope. Then, he saw the price.

"It's too much," he mumbled. He told Harold how much he could spend. Harold refused to give up. He went on with his search.

"What about a suitcase?" Harold asked.

"A suitcase!" said Ben. "But I just told you what I could spend. There's no way I could afford a suitcase."

"Ah, but there's where you're wrong," Harold said, smiling. "Here we have it, the perfect choice. A collapsing suitcase. When folded, it's only the size of a pair of shoes. But it unfolds to carry home all those mementos from your trip. A truly unique gift. And a bargain at nineteen ninety-five."

"Let me see that, Harold." Ben thought his friend was joking. To his joy, Harold was not. He had found it! He was sure Chuck and Louisa didn't have one. He knew they would have things to bring back. And, best of all, he could afford it.

"How will I get it?" he asked Harold. "Do you think I can mail the money to the store? Do you think the store will wrap it?"

"Whoa, there!" Harold laughed. "One question at a time. I don't know any more than you. We'll have to find out."

Carefully, the two men planned. Ben would call the store. He would see whether he could pay by mail. Also, he'd ask if they delivered. He'd check on gift wrapping, too.

There was one big problem in all this. The phone was on the table in the hall. Ben didn't want Mrs. Brandon to hear him make the call. He didn't want her to tease him. He'd have to wait until Mrs. Brandon was out.

On Wednesday, Ben got his chance. Mrs. Brandon had gone shopping. Harold was still asleep. John was at work.

Ben had no trouble calling the store. The salesman was very polite. But he was also very sure. He said that he was sorry, but it could not be done. Now, with a charge account, of course, it would be simple. But sending cash—well, it simply was not done.

Disgusted, Ben slammed down the phone. Harold was just coming out of his room. Ben told him what had happened.

"You should have asked to speak to the manager," Harold said.

Ben dialed again. To his surprise, Harold's advice worked. The manager was glad to help.

"We can send the package C.O.D.," he said. "You pay for it when it's delivered. But we don't provide gift wrapping."

Ben ordered the gift over the phone. The manager said it would arrive in about a week. Ben thanked him happily.

Chapter 6

On Wednesday night, after supper, Chuck stopped by. Ben was glad to see him. It was hard not to hint about the present. It was even harder when Chuck mentioned the trip.

"Less than a month to go!" he said to Ben. "Then, we'll be away from it all. That's hard to believe, isn't it? Especially on a cold and rainy night like this."

"I just hope it doesn't rain on your trip," Ben commented.

"It wouldn't dare!" Chuck replied. Ben hoped not. Louisa had certainly earned a good rest. She worked harder than anyone he knew.

"Who's going to take care of the kids?" Ben asked.

"Louisa's mother," said Chuck. "She's coming early, to learn the ropes. Oh, that reminds me, Ben. Louisa wants to see you before we leave."

Ben smiled. "I'd like to see Louisa and the kids. And you, too, of course."

"Would a Saturday be good for you, then?" Chuck asked.

"Sure," Ben said.

"We'll plan on it, then," said Chuck. "We'll let you know when."

Ben was pleased. This weekend, at least, he would have something to do. It would be good to get out for a change.

* * *

Saturday arrived. It was almost noon. Ben had not heard from Chuck yet. Harold was going to lunch. He stuck his head in at Ben's door.

"You still here? I thought you were going to your brother's."

"So did I," Ben said. "But I still haven't heard from him."

"Well, it's Saturday," Harold consoled him. "Bet they slept in. They'll call pretty soon."

"I guess you're right," Ben said. He didn't sound convinced, though. "Guess I may as well come to lunch."

"A good choice," Harold said. "As I always say, when all else fails—"

"Eat!" Ben finished for him. The two men went in to lunch together.

By three o'clock, Ben had given up. Chuck must have forgotten. Ben tried not to care, but it didn't work. He had been so excited about going. Now, he felt like a fool. He wished he hadn't told Mrs. Brandon. But how could he know this would happen? Anyway, there was nothing to do now. He closed the door to his room and lay down on his bed.

Ben awoke to knocking.

"Who is it?" Ben called sleepily.

"It's Mrs. Brandon, Benny," the answer came. "May I come in?"

"I'm sleeping," he complained.

As he had feared, she came in, anyway. She sat in the chair by his bed, looking concerned.

"Benny, have you heard from Chuck?" she questioned.

Inside, Ben was angry. What business was it of hers? But, aloud, he said simply, "No."

"Then don't you think you should call him?" she went on.

"No," he said stubbornly.

"Well, if *you* won't, *I* will," she said. She ignored Ben's protests. Before he could get up, she had Chuck on the line.

Ben felt about four years old. Mrs. Brandon had not listened to him. She had just gone ahead and done what she wanted to do. "For his own good," no doubt.

In a minute, Mrs. Brandon was at his door again.

"Benny," she begged. "Chuck is so upset! It was all a mix-up. He wants to talk to you."

"I don't want to talk to him. Go away and leave me alone!" Ben exclaimed.

Mrs. Brandon sighed. She returned to the phone. Soon, she was back.

"He says if you won't talk, he'll come over," she said.

That was the last thing Ben wanted. As it was, he had almost no pride left. If he saw Chuck now, he'd lose the rest. He'd have to talk to him.

"Tell him I'm coming," he muttered.

* * *

It was very simple, really. Chuck had said *some* Saturday, not *this* Saturday. Ben could tell that Chuck felt awful. In the end, Chuck put Louisa on the phone. Talking to her helped. She talked Ben into coming the next Saturday for Bud's Little League game. There was a picnic afterwards. She made it seem like a favor to her. Ben was grateful for that. After today, his pride needed all the help it could get.

Ben hung up the phone. Then, he headed for the porch. There was still a little daylight left.

Ben sat in a chair on the porch. Harold spoke briefly to him on his way out. Inside the house, the phone rang. Everyone seemed to have places to go. Ben wondered if they knew how lucky they were.

A voice broke into his thoughts. It was Susie, the little girl from next door. She was standing by the fence. Ben's heart went out to her. He decided to be friendly this time. After all, she was only a child. She hadn't meant to hurt his feelings.

"Hi there, Susie!" he called.

"Can I come over?" she asked.

Ben paused. He had only meant to be friendly. He didn't want to start a childcare service. Still, Susie looked lonely. And he wasn't so busy himself.

"All right," Ben agreed. "But just for a minute." Happily, the child squeezed through the fence. In no time, she was seated in a chair across from Ben. Her legs dangled high above the ground. She sat straight and proud.

Susie told Ben she was the youngest of three daughters. All three lived next door with their mother, who was divorced. Susie's two sisters were teenagers. They had little time for her. Her mother often worked late and came home

very tired. Mostly, Susie played by herself. She watched a lot of TV.

"But now," she said, "I've got a friend. You will be my friend, won't you, Mister Ben?"

"Yes," Ben said slowly, "but I don't have too much time—"

Susie seemed not to hear. "We can talk, like today. We can play, too. And you can read my storybooks to me. I hardly ever get to hear them. Won't you, please?"

Ben was taken aback. He felt sorry for Susie. But he didn't want her over every day—even if he did have time. He shouldn't have to raise someone else's kid. He had problems enough of his own.

"Susie," he said, "I'm too old to be your friend. I wouldn't be much fun. And how could I read to you? Sometimes you can't understand what I say. You'd better find somebody else."

Susie looked very serious. "Oh, no, Mister Ben. I think you're fun. And I understand you OK, now. Please be my friend?"

"Sorry, Susie," said Ben. "I have to go in now."

"Can I come back tomorrow?" she asked.

"I'm busy tomorrow," Ben lied.

"But when?" Susie looked hopeful.

"We'll see," Ben said vaguely. "Now, you'd better go home."

As he spoke, Susie frowned. Sadly, she got out of the chair and left the porch.

It was the best thing to do, Ben told himself. He didn't need a little kid hanging around. His mind agreed, but his heart did not. Ben felt even lonelier than before. Stubbornly, he tried to shrug it off. He picked up the paper and began to read.

Chapter 7

A week later, on Saturday, Ben woke up early. He felt excited. Today was the ball game and picnic with Chuck's family.

He glanced out the window. It looked like a perfect day. It was still early, but he decided to get up.

Slowly and carefully, he sat up in bed. Painfully, he slid his legs across the sheet. As he did this, his left arm shot out to the side. His water glass flew off the table. It shattered loudly on the floor.

Ben swore to himself. He put on his slippers and kicked the glass into a corner. He knew he would cut himself if he tried to clean it up.

After he was dressed, Ben sat back down on his bed. It was only six-thirty. Half an hour till breakfast. He decided to get out his clothes for the game. He planned to bathe after breakfast. He wanted to look his best.

Bathing was always a problem for Ben. He couldn't get himself into the tub. A shower stall was easier. But the boarding house didn't have one. Ben was forced to rely on Harold's help. Often, Harold was out when Ben needed him. Other times, he was asleep. But today, Harold had promised. Ben had made sure of that.

* * *

It was half past ten. Ben had eaten, read the paper, and made his bed. He'd even sat on the porch for a while. But there was no sign of Harold. It looked as if Ben would have to wake him up after all.

Ben knocked loudly on the door to Harold's room. He heard Harold's sleepy groan.

"What do you want?" Harold mumbled.

"Sorry, Harold. I have to start my bath now. It's ten-thirty."

"Oh, all right!" sighed Harold. "I'm on my way. Just give me a minute to wake up."

Ben made his way back to the bathroom. Then, he sat on the toilet seat to wait. He listened. He couldn't hear a sound from Harold's room. Better give him time, Ben thought.

The clock on the wall read 11 o'clock. Ben couldn't wait any longer. He made his way back to the hall. He pounded on Harold's door again.

"Harold! You've *got* to come! Now!"

"Huh? Oh, yeah. Sorry, Ben. Be right there." Once more, Ben started towards the bathroom. This time, Harold beat him to the tub.

"C'mon, Ben. Let's get this over with," Harold said with a yawn. "Then, I can get back to the sack. I intend to sleep all day."

Holding onto the sink, Ben got out of his clothes. Harold helped Ben into the tub. "You'll need me to get you out, too, won't you?" he asked.

"Yes," Ben admitted. Harold always asked that. Harold sat down on the toilet seat. "Guess I'll just wait here," he said.

Ben sighed to himself. He wished he could take a bath without bothering anyone. And it sure would be nice to have some privacy. But, no matter. He wouldn't think about things like that today.

* * *

Ben barely made it to lunch on time. He didn't eat much. He was too worried about spilling something on his shirt.

After lunch, he sat by the window to watch for Chuck. Soon, he saw him coming down the walk. Louisa and the boys were in the car. Ben began struggling to his feet. As he did, he heard Mrs. Brandon's voice coming from outside.

"So nice of you and your wife. Poor thing, he gets out so little. I can hardly find time to take him anywhere. And that chair of his is heavy. Well, I'm sure Benny will enjoy his treat."

"Thanks, Mrs. Brandon," said Chuck. "I know you do all you can for him."

Ben fumed. "Poor little Benny," indeed. He was sick of the way she treated him. Just like a little boy. And Chuck, too.

When Chuck came in, Ben managed to smile. He tried to put his anger aside. Soon, they were headed for the ballpark.

* * *

As soon as Chuck stopped the car, Bud shot out. He ran to join his teammates. They were on the field, warming up.

Chip ran off to watch. He was wearing a baseball cap. He even carried a mitt. He couldn't play until next year.

Chuck pushed Ben over to the bleachers. Louisa walked alongside. Then, Chuck left to join the other fathers.

"How's it going, Ben?" Louisa asked.

"Not too bad," he told her. "It'll never be like home. But the people are pretty nice. Especially a guy named Harold. It's sure a lot better than Rest Haven."

Louisa nodded. "Are you finding more to do?"

"A little," Ben said. "But I'd sure like to get out more. A bus comes right by the house, if I could only get on it."

"That reminds me," said Louisa. "The city is starting a bus service for handicapped and older people."

Ben's eyes lit up. "Wouldn't that be great? Then I could get around town. Who knows, maybe I might even find a job somewhere."

"I work for the city, you know," said Louisa. "I'll ask my boss when the new buses start running."

Ben was excited. He wanted to ask Louisa more. But the game was about to begin.

A whistle blew. All the boys ran off the field. The team bench was close to Louisa and Ben's seats. The players talked excitedly. Ben

could hear snatches of what they said.
Suddenly, he listened more closely. They were
talking about him.

"Hey, Bud, who's that?" cried one of the
boys.

Bud mumbled, "My Uncle Benny."

"Hey, I didn't know you had an uncle who was a retard!"

"He's not! You take that back, or you'll be sorry!"

"OK, OK. So he's not a retard. But, you got to admit, he looks weird."

Ben sighed. He hated to embarrass Bud.

Louisa squeezed Ben's hand. "Just ignore them," she advised. "They don't know any better."

Ben smiled weakly. The whistle blew again. Time for the game to begin. Chuck and Chip joined Ben and Louisa. Together, they watched the game.

Ben had never been to a baseball game before. But he had watched a lot on TV. This was not the same at all, he thought. The field looked much smaller, and there was no scoreboard. Most of all, the pitching was slower. The crowd was smaller, but seemed just as excited. Ben was excited, too. He wanted to clap and cheer for Bud's team, but he didn't. He thought he might look or sound funny.

Bud's team lost, but not by much. Bud played well, Ben thought. He got two hits. Still, they had not won. Bud looked close to tears when he joined his family.

"You were great, Bud," said Chip loyally.

"Not great enough," Bud complained. He kicked the ground.

"You can't always win," Louisa reminded him. "Let's go get a picnic table."

"I'm not hungry," Bud sighed.

"Well, I am!" said Chip. He ran off towards the picnic area.

Louisa pushed Ben's chair. Chuck and Bud walked ahead, discussing the game. Chuck had his arm around his son's shoulder. Ben felt suddenly sad.

That's something I'll never have, he thought to himself. A wife and kids. He sighed deeply. Then, he looked up. Louisa was talking. She was introducing him to one of their neighbors. He said hello shyly.

Louisa pushed him over to where Chuck, Bud, and Chip were sitting. Some of the fathers grilled hamburgers. The food tasted great to Ben. It had been years since his mother had grilled hamburgers outside.

But something else was like old times, too. Ben dripped catsup all down his shirt front. He tried to laugh it off.

Bud and Chip giggled. Chuck looked upset. But Louisa's smile made Ben feel better.

The talk during the meal was lively, and Bud was soon back in good spirits. Chuck and Louisa talked about their trip.

"Married ten years, and this will be our first trip alone," Louisa said. "That's some anniversary present."

"Uncle Benny," said Chip, "Bud and I are making something really neat for Mom and Dad. It's a surprise. What're you getting them?"

"Chip!" Louisa scolded. "Your Uncle Benny doesn't have to get us anything."

"That's OK, Louisa," Ben assured her. He wanted to say more. He didn't, though. It had to be a surprise.

* * *

Chuck dropped Ben off after the picnic. "See you soon," Chuck had said. Ben smiled to himself. If his plans worked out, they *would*. He would invite them over to pick up their present. He reached into the drawer by his side and pulled out the ad.

"They'll like it," he said to himself. "And I'm sure they'll be surprised."

He put the ad back in the drawer. Then, he settled down in his chair by the window.

Chapter 8

The package arrived in the middle of the week. Ben was sitting on the porch by himself. It was almost lunchtime.

"C.O.D. package for Ben Hollister," the mail carrier said.

"That's me," said Ben. "If you can wait a minute, I'll get your money."

Ben hurried into the house. The money was in his top drawer. He paid the mail carrier and took the package straight to his room. But there was no time to open it. Mrs. Brandon was calling everyone to lunch.

* * *

After lunch, Ben headed back to his room. The suitcase was a beauty. He loved to look at it. Later, he showed it to Harold, too. His friend was properly impressed. And it was Harold who first thought of the card.

"A card!" Ben repeated dumbly. "I'd forgotten about that. And the gift has to be wrapped, too. That means paper and ribbon. Not to mention scissors, tape, and who knows what all. I've never wrapped a package in my life. Have you, Harold?"

"I'm not exactly a pro," said Harold.

"That's all right," said Ben. "Will you help me? And can you get a card, if I give you the money? What about paper and ribbon? Can you get that, too?"

"Say no more," Harold replied. "I'll be glad to do it. After all, what are friends for?"

"It'll have to be soon, though, Harold," Ben nagged. "They're leaving in three days! Can you do it tomorrow?"

"No problem," Harold assured him. "Tomorrow it is. And now, to bed. Got to get my beauty sleep, you know."

"Me, too," Ben grinned. "Thanks, Harold."

Ben was pleased, but also worried. Harold was not always trustworthy. Sometimes, he forgot things, especially on "meeting" nights.

Ben now knew that Harold's "meetings" were trips to local bars. And when he drank, Harold wasn't himself.

* * *

Sure enough, Harold did have a "meeting" the next night. Before he left, Ben reminded him about the card. Harold assured him that he would get one. There was a store on the way, he told him. Ben gave his friend the money, hoping for the best.

By 10 o'clock that night, Harold still had not come home. Ben was frantic. He thought of calling the bar. He had no way of knowing which one Harold was at, though. Besides, he didn't want to make his friend mad.

Just as Ben had given up, the door opened loudly. Harold was singing. Ben shuddered. So much for my card, he thought.

"'Lo, Benny," Harold said.

He *must* be drunk, Ben thought. He knows I hate to be called Benny.

"Don' you wanna see it?" Harold inquired.

"See what?" Ben said hopelessly.

"The card, silly. Gotcha yer card. Said I would. Good one, too." Harold reached into his coat pocket and handed the card to Ben.

"I can't send *this* to Louisa!" Ben cried.

"'S funny!" Harold insisted.

"Not to me," Ben mourned. "And I'm sure Louisa wouldn't think so, either."

Harold looked offended. "Whatsa matter with sex?" he asked, staggering backwards.

"Nothing, Harold," Ben said. "I just don't want it on my card."

Harold was pouting. "Do a guy a favor, and whaddya get?"

"I know, Harold, and I'm sorry," Ben said. "I just can't use that card. Would you please get me another one? You know I'd do it myself if I could."

"I know," Harold said slowly. "All right. I'll do it tomorrow. Now g'night, Benny. These legs won't hold out much longer." He started towards his room.

"Harold, wait!" Ben called after his friend. "What about the paper and ribbon?"

"'Morrow!" Harold groaned, as his door slammed shut.

Chapter 9

Ben had fallen asleep worrying. He was still worrying when he woke up. Chuck and Louisa were leaving the next morning. He had to get the present to them on time.

About three-thirty, Ben saw Harold. He was dressed to go out. Ben was puzzled. Most days, Harold only went out at night. He liked to sleep all morning. In the afternoon, he worked around the house.

"Where are you going, Harold?" Ben asked.

"Gotta take care of some business," he answered. Before Ben could question him further, he was out the door. Ben waited for his return.

Harold came home just before dinner. "Got your stuff, old chap," he said gruffly. He handed a bag to Ben.

After last night, Ben was afraid to hope. He looked at the card. It was fine. Reaching back into the bag, he pulled out paper and ribbon. Harold had done it!

"I said I'd do it." Harold sounded hurt.

"I know you did, Harold. I don't know how to thank you. I never could have done it without your help," Ben replied.

"Never mind that," said Harold. "Let's go have dinner. Then, we can get on with the wrapping."

"But what about your meeting?" Ben asked.

"No meeting tonight," Harold informed him. "Conflict of interest."

"Harold, you're some friend!" Ben glowed.

Harold just grinned. The two men went in to eat.

* * *

Sure enough, Harold was no expert. They didn't have any tape, either. But, with much effort, they managed to wrap the gift. Ben was pleased with the way it looked. Bursting with pride, he called Chuck. Chuck was busy. He even sounded annoyed.

"I would, Benny, but we're just swamped. It's almost nine, and I'm not even packed. You know we have to leave first thing in the morning. What a time to call. We just don't have time to see you right now."

"But—" Ben started. Then he stopped. He couldn't tell Chuck why he needed to see him.

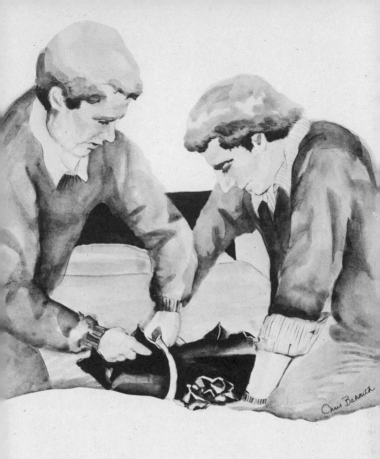

And the present wouldn't be any good when they got back. He'd gotten it for their trip.

"I'll call you back," Ben told his brother firmly.

"Benny, I told you, I can't—" Chuck began.

Ben hung up. He marvelled at himself. He had never hung up on anyone before.

Squaring his shoulders, he started towards Harold's room. Ben hated to ask any more of his friend. But he needed help.

Harold agreed to help him. Ben gave Harold Chuck's address, and Harold went out to wait for a bus. Ben went into the living room. He tried to read, but soon gave it up.

All Ben's thoughts were on the gift. He tried to figure out when Harold would arrive. He imagined him giving the present to Chuck and Louisa. They would call when they got it, he was sure. He couldn't wait to talk to Louisa. She would be so surprised. He wondered what she would say.

* * *

Ben awoke with a start. He had fallen asleep. Can't sleep now, he scolded himself. Got to stay awake for the call. He looked at his watch. Almost 11 o'clock! Chuck and Louisa must have gotten the present by now. So why hadn't they called? And where was Harold?

Ben felt sick at heart. Maybe Harold had gotten sidetracked. Maybe he had decided to go to his "meeting," after all.

Still, Ben refused to give up hope. They'd call. He was sure they would.

Chapter 10

Somewhere close by, Ben could hear whistling. Harold's back, he thought sleepily. He opened his eyes. To his surprise, the room was full of light. The whistling was the teakettle, not Harold. It was morning. Mrs. Brandon was fixing breakfast.

No wonder he was stiff, Ben thought. He had fallen asleep in the living room chair. Slowly, the truth hit him. Chuck and Louisa were gone! And they hadn't called.

Ben couldn't believe it. He felt a sob rise in his throat. I never should have tried, he thought bitterly. I should have known it wouldn't work.

Just then, Mrs. Brandon came in.

"So you're awake, Benny. I saw you there this morning when I came down. Just like my Johnny. Well, breakfast is ready. Come and eat, before your pancakes get cold."

Mrs. Brandon started to take Ben's arm, but he brushed her aside. "I'm not hungry," he choked out. He started to get up.

"Well, I'll be!" Mrs. Brandon exclaimed. "And I thought you'd be so happy that I made pancakes. Guess I'll just eat them myself." She sighed loudly. "Try to make a special treat, and what thanks do I get?"

Ben could not speak. His throat was too tight, and his eyes were full of tears. He went to his room and sat on the bed.

There was a knock on his door. Just who I don't need, he thought fiercely. He pretended not to hear. The knocking persisted.

"Who is it?" he called.

"Benny," said Mrs. Brandon. "I have a note for you. It was on the front door. I just found it when I went out for the mail."

Ben sat up. "Bring it in," he said tensely.

Mrs. Brandon put the note in his hand. Then, she turned and left the room.

"Dear Ben," the note said. "We called you late last night. A man named John answered and said you were asleep. We just couldn't leave without thanking you. The suitcase is great! We've never seen anything like it before. It will be perfect for bringing back souvenirs. Chuck wants to stick in a native girl! I'm standing firm, though.

"Got to go now to catch the plane. We'll call you when we return. Much love always, Louisa and Chuck."

Ben felt proud and happy. His present was a success. And he'd done it all on his own. Or, at least, almost on his own. He could never have gotten the gift without Harold.

Harold wouldn't have gone to so much trouble for most people, Ben knew. I guess he really likes me, Ben concluded.

Even Mrs. Brandon was a friend, he guessed. In her own way, she cared about him. She hurt his feelings at times. He knew she didn't mean to, though. As for himself, he was growing fond of "Mother Bee."

Just then, Ben's stomach growled. He remembered Mrs. Brandon's offer of breakfast. "Mother Bee!" he called.

His door opened at once. She must have been right behind it. She stood in the doorway, a worried look on her face. Ben felt a rush of warmth towards her. He'd tell her, he decided. He'd tell her about the gift.

"Mother Bee," he said. "Does that offer of pancakes still stand?"

She looked surprised. "I guess it does," she said.

"Well, then," said Ben. "I'd like to accept. And I'd like to tell you what all this is about."

Mrs. Brandon smiled. "I'd like that," she admitted. "I have been wondering a bit."

Ben was sure she wondered more than just a bit. He chuckled.

"Better make plenty," he warned her. "I think I could eat at least ten."

* * *

After breakfast, Ben was still excited. He didn't want to go back to his room. The morning was sunny, so he went out to sit on the porch. He saw Susie standing near the fence. He smiled at her. She looked surprised, but pleased.

"Hi, Mister Ben," she called shyly. "Can I come see you?"

Ben hesitated just a moment. "I guess so," he said. "Sure."

Susie didn't waste any time. She was over the fence in a flash.

"Wait a minute, Susie," said Ben.

She stopped, a hurt look on her face. But Ben was quick to explain.

"Susie, why don't you get a few books first? I'll read to you. That's what you wanted, wasn't it?"

Susie brightened. Without stopping to speak, she dashed back to her house.

Cute little girl, Ben thought to himself. And nobody to play with. Well, today she's got me. I've got her, too, come to think of it. And Harold and Mrs. Brandon. I guess I've got a family, after all. I never realized how lucky I am. I've been feeling sorry for myself all this time for nothing.

Ben sat back. I've sure come a long way since Rest Haven, he thought.

Seven series of good books for all readers:

WRITERS' VOICES
Selections from the works of America's finest and most popular writers, along with background information, maps, and other supplementary materials. Authors include: Kareem Abdul-Jabbar • Maya Angelou • Bill Cosby • Alex Haley • Stephen King • Loretta Lynn • Larry McMurtry • Amy Tan • Anne Tyler • Abigail Van Buren • Alice Walker • Tom Wolfe, and many others.

NEW WRITERS' VOICES
Anthologies and individual narratives by adult learners. A wide range of topics includes home and family, prison life, and meeting challenges. Many titles contain photographs or illustrations.

OURWORLD
Selections from the works of well-known science writers, along with related articles and illustrations. Authors include David Attenborough and Carl Sagan.

FOR YOUR INFORMATION
Clearly written and illustrated works on important self-help topics. Subjects include: Eating Right • Managing Stress • Getting Fit • About AIDS • Getting Good Health Care, among others.

TIMELESS TALES
Classic myths, legends, folk tales, and other stories from around the world, with special illustrations.

SPORTS
Fact-filled books on baseball, football, basketball, and boxing, with lots of action photos. With read-along tapes narrated by Phil Rizzuto, Frank Gifford, Dick Vitale, and Sean O'Grady.

SULLY GOMEZ MYSTERIES
Fast-paced detective series starring Sully Gomez and the streets of Los Angeles.

WRITE FOR OUR FREE COMPLETE CATALOG:

Signal Hill Publications
P.O. Box 131
Syracuse, NY 13210-0131